Nine till Five

Dale Robertson

Copyright © 2016 Dale Robertson

dalerobertson.co.uk
https://twitter.com/Dale_Dez81

The right of Dale Robertson to be identified as the Author of this Work has been asserted by him in accordance with the Copyright, Designs and Patents Act 1988.

All rights reserved. No part of this book may be reproduced in any form or by any electronic means, including information storage and retrieval systems, without written permission from the author, except for the purposes of review.

This is a work of fiction. Names, characters, businesses, places, events and incidents are either the product of the author's imagination or used in a fictitious manner. Any resemblance to actual persons, living or dead, or events is purely coincidental.

Cover Art by David Phee.

PROLOGUE
1912

The man might have been strapped to the bed but he still gave Edward the creeps. Monreith Asylum housed some of the sickest individuals in the country, and this guy, Thomas, was certainly near the top of the list, if not, sitting at the pinnacle.

He was moved here from a high-security facility in the city following an incident that left the warden and his staff in complete shock, in which he pulled a fellow convict's eyeballs out of his head and proceeded to eat them. The guards were so stunned at first they didn't quite know what to do. They had seen lots of terrible things; rapes and stabbings and the like, but nothing quite as brutal as this. However, they quickly regained their senses and called upon the riot squad guys.

But as the squad moved towards Thomas, he didn't move. He simply sat where he was, staring at the staff blankly, mouth dripping with fluid from the half-chewed eyes. The hardened professionals had said that the way in which he remained so calm was the strangest thing they had ever seen. Unnerved them, they said.

It paled in comparison to his original crime.

He had been convicted of killing his family—a wife and child—in the most horrific fashion imaginable.

He had forced his wife to watch as he slit his son's throat, smiling insanely throughout. Before the blood had even stopped spurting, he'd sliced hunks of flesh off the boy and ate it raw. His wife had vomited instantly at the appalling scene before her, and Thomas had rushed towards her in a rage, battering her to death with the nearest available object—a glass ornament.

The police were called by the neighbours, due to the excessive noise, and had walked into a bloodbath. Thomas was sitting at the middle of the room, chewing and slurping, the bodies of his family lying next to him, half stripped of flesh.

"Come in, join the party," Thomas had said, jovially, as if it was the most normal thing in the world.

His reason? —the Devil told him to.

The arresting officers, and the guards in the prison thereafter, treated him as if he were the Devil incarnate. They did their best to steer clear of him if they could. He never threatened them, or spoke aggressively, but to them, that was worse.

He had a habit of staring. If he stared at you, it was as if he was looking right into your soul. And sometimes, if you were extremely unlucky, he would wink or smile. It was enough to send a shiver down the spines of the most experienced of staff.

Following the prison episode, he was transferred to the Asylum. A place where depraved individuals were locked up and forgotten about. Unfortunately for Edward, it was his job to *look after* them. Him and the rest of the personnel.

Thomas wasn't alone at Monreith; there were plenty of other hideous individuals to keep him company, people who should never have been near society in the first place and would never be again. Brutal rapists, arsonists, and murderers. Most claimed insanity, that Satan himself had whispered sweet nothings in their ears. Others openly admitted that they enjoyed hurting others, all the while laughing about the horrible crimes they had committed, as if it was a cheery party anecdote.

Edward had worked there for several years, and had grown accustomed to the monsters inhabiting Monreith. It had certainly been difficult to begin with. During the first few weeks of his tenure he had nearly quit on several occasions, but he needed the money, so stuck at it.

Several of the workers would happily beat and berate the inmates, safe in the knowledge that they were strapped to a bed. Acting tough when they knew they were guarded from retaliation. Edward would never partake in the assaults, though sometimes he stood outside the door as the unwarranted punishment was meted out. Other times, fellow staff members would make him stand in the room and watch. The patients—Edward often laughed at the term—would just look on, never taking their eyes off their tormentors, but also never reacting.

Something about that unsettled Edward. He often wondered what grisly fantasies they were conjuring up behind those glaring eyes. There was a hidden darkness there that didn't belong to this world.

Edward began to wheel the bed from the room and down the hall. Thick wooden doors, with iron-barred windows, littered either side of the corridor, behind which lived the various abnormalities.

Edward kept his eyes straight ahead, trying to ignore the assorted threats and obscenities emanating from each room. He continued down the hall to the private room, to where the priest was waiting.

This wasn't an unusual event; the bosses encouraged priests to visit the patients to show they were at least *trying* to help the 'animals'. Much of the time, the priest was met with a torrent of curses and suggestions of acts that would befall them and any family they had. Some priests—the strong ones—persisted month after month, but many never returned.

Arriving at the room, Edward stopped and opened the door. There were two guards and a priest present. The stone room was empty, except for a small table that the priest had placed a bag upon. Edward frowned as he stared at the bag. *That's slightly unusual*, he thought. *They normally just bring a bible.*

Edward's eyes moved up to the three men standing opposite him. He nodded.

"Bring him in," the priest said.

Edward pushed the bed to the middle of the room so that the three men stood at the head of it. The guards parted, took up position either side of the bed, with the priest remaining at the head.

"Thank you. I'll knock on the door when I'm finished," said the priest.

Edward hesitated for a second before replying. "Erm… okay. I'll just be right outside."

He turned and left the room, closing the door behind him and locking it.

*

Edwards' head had started to loll with fatigue as he leaned back against the wall. He stepped forward and shook each leg in turn, trying to banish the pins and needles, whilst scanning left and right along the long corridor.

"They're not normally this long," he muttered to himself.

He was about to turn to the door and unlock it when he heard two, long drawn-out noises coming from inside the room. He paused, not sure if it was just his imagination playing tricks on him. He reached for the key and slid it into the lock. His other hand went to the viewing port in the door and slid the barrier across.

The priest's face was right there, eyes staring blankly through Edward. Edward's heart caught in his mouth.

He automatically turned the key, a subconscious act that he had performed hundreds of times before. This time, it took his brain a few seconds to catch up, by which time it was too late.

Far too late.

As the lock clicked open, the door swung outwards, knocking Edward back. The priest was somehow launched towards him, and he fell to the ground with the dead man's body on top of him.

His mind couldn't comprehend what was happening, but as Edward panicked and writhed beneath the corpse, he felt some strange, sticky substance upon his palms. Lifting them to his face he could see, through the gloom, it was blood.

His heart began to race, and he started to hyperventilate at the unholy event that his brain was now accepting as real. Before he had a chance to react, the body was yanked unceremoniously off him by unseen hands. In its place, the monster—who should be strapped to a gurney in the room with the open door—sitting on his chest, staring deep into his eyes with a grin that bordered mischievous and manic.

"You're all going to pay, piggy," the man growled.

He grabbed Edward by the ears and began to bash his head down on the floor. Edward's vision began to blur as his mind, figuratively and literally, began to break.

The monster stopped for a brief second before lunging forward and sinking his teeth into Edward's neck and pulling a chunk of flesh away. Edward tried to speak, but only a gurgle came, a spittle of blood escaping his lips.

The maniac jumped off his chest and began rummaging through his pockets, seemingly finding what he was looking for.

He jangled the keys in front of Edward's ebbing eyes, let out a hideous laugh, and darted off towards the other cell doors.

As the life seeped out of him, Edward could only watch as each door was opened. The escaping fiends emerged from their cells, glanced both ways, and saw him lying there vulnerable.

They rushed towards him.

His vision faded to black before his body succumbed to another assault.

*

Unofficial report from an anonymous source:

The beginning of the end for Monreith Asylum happened as soon as the first inmate escaped. He and the other prisoners had unleashed a living hell on the staff, especially the ones who took pleasure in beating them. They didn't stand a chance. They got too arrogant; they thought no-one could break free. Thinking that way, they didn't have many procedures in place should that event arise. Authorities had stated that a fire had been started somehow. Whether by accident or on purpose, they weren't sure, but the place was destroyed. By the time they got to recording bodies, not all patients were accounted for. Some remained missing.

1
PRESENT DAY - MONDAY

"Jesus Christ! How can these people not understand a simple word for a password?" Damien vented to no-one in particular as he put the phone down. "I mean, come on. These people teach our kids, for fuck's sake."

It was the same old issue when it was his turn to work on the Help Desk, helping stupid people. They never seemed to want to help themselves; they just phoned up, expected assistance without any manners or grace, then hung up without any thanks.

Ignorant fucks.

It took all of Damien's willpower not to let loose with a string of choice, colourful words for the customers. He closed his eyes for five seconds and let out a huge sigh, which garnered the attention of his nearby colleagues. Picking up his coffee cup, he stood from his chair and headed out of the office towards the tearoom.

Walking along the lengthy corridor, he glanced out of each large window as they passed, admiring the scenic view set out before him. The location of the building was nice, away from the hustle and bustle of town life, good places to take a walk, and a nice feeling of serenity within the gardens that lay scattered around the vast grounds. He took in the view of the church off in the distance.

He was daydreaming, but at the end of the corridor he subconsciously lifted his hand to push open the upcoming door. He was abruptly brought back to reality as his hand touched nothing and he stumbled forward.

Craig, one of his co-workers, stood there with his fist wrapped around the handle, the door half open, and a look of fright on his face.

"Fucking hell, Damo. You scared the shit out of me."

"I scared you? Fuck, man. I thought my heart was going to stop," Damien replied.

As he composed himself and tried to calm his erratic heartbeat, Craig and he burst into laughter. "They need to put a window in this door so you can see if anyone is on the other side."

"Health and Safety issue, innit. Need to do something, this happens a lot."

Continuing his break-time journey, Damien passed the water cooler and entered the kitchen.

"Alright, folks?" he said, as he noticed Grant standing against the wall and Nina stirring two cups of tea. Grant smiled and nodded in his general direction.

"Hey, Damien. You alright today?" Nina asked.

"Good, thanks. Well, apart from having to speak to idiots on the phone all day."

Grant and Nina chuckled.

"Hey," Nina continued, "did you hear what happened the other night? The cleaner that works here?"

"The weird one? No, I haven't heard anything. What's happened?" Damien asked.

Grant chipped in, "Apparently he quit last night. Just walked right out. Well, more like he ran."

"Ran? What are you talking about?" Damien asked.

"Well, *apparently*," Nina raised her eyebrows, "he got spooked out cleaning the office. The care call staff heard a scream and went to investigate. They found him cowering under a desk, babbling nonsense. They couldn't calm him down, either, and he bolted out the door, shouting about the place being haunted."

"Wow. I've heard stories about this place but nothing's ever happened to anyone I know. He was a bit strange anyway, though. Are you sure your story is right?"

"That's what I heard from the girls downstairs."

"Cool. I love shit like that. Might have to stay late one night, see if I can spot me some ghosties," Damien said, giggling.

Nina glared at him. "You'll be here on your own. We won't be staying with you, that's for sure. Especially with these dark nights."

"Hear, hear!" Grant agreed.

Damien smirked as he finished stirring sugar into his coffee. "Chicken."

Grant and Nina feigned laughter, picked up their mugs, and bid Damien a curt, "See ya," as they left the kitchen, leaving Damien to his own thoughts.

He walked across to the window and placed his chin in his hands, propping himself up with his elbows, staring at the tall oak tree blowing in the wind. He laughed to himself, "Must have been quite the scare, poor cleaner."

He picked up his coffee cup and headed back to his desk.

*

Damien pulled his tired eyes away from the screen and glanced at the clock on the wall—17:30. He logged off his machine and started to pack up the things lying on the desk.

Finally, home time.

As he stood to put his jacket on, he suddenly realised how quiet the office was. He looked around and saw that no-one else was there. He began to wonder how he had missed his colleagues leaving. Had he been that engrossed in work?

It was a large open plan office, and sound carried well (sometimes a little too well), but the only sound he could hear now was the dull *hum* of the air conditioning fans built into the high ceilings.

He wandered over to the control panel on the wall and switched the fans off. They slowed to a halt and the open space was plunged into total silence. So quiet you could have heard an ant fart. Damien stood still for a few moments, soaking up the lull. He was so used to the constant noise that surrounded his day-to-day work that the calmness was eerie. He felt the hair on the nape of his neck stand on end. He shuddered and moved back to his desk, picking up his jacket and slipping it on.

As he made his way to the exit, he froze. He was sure he could hear the faint tapping of keys on a keyboard. A noise that certainly wasn't there a second ago but, his mind told him, could just be coincidental. He turned anyway and doublechecked the office. *Definitely no-one here.* He decided to take a quick look through the archway separating his office from the business side of things. They had an office of similar size and layout, but when he took a step back and peered through the arch, he couldn't see anyone there either.

"Maybe someone round the far corner," he muttered to himself. He shrugged and left.

As he walked along the hall, he passed the familiar windows and looked out, an automatic reaction no matter how hard not to. Darkness blanketed the exterior world, apart from the light from a lone lamppost on the path snaking up to the car park, which allowed him to see the start of the route leading in the opposite direction alongside the building.

As he passed one window, he thought he caught sight of someone standing there, a shadow near the lamppost just beyond illumination. But by the time he arrived at the next window, it was gone, if it had ever been there to begin with.

He frowned, but kept walking to the next, his eyes focused on outside. Still nothing.

"Nina and her ghost stories," he said, laughing.

Pushing open the door at the end of the corridor, Damien sauntered through the adjoining hallway, looking in each empty room as he passed. He made it to the door opening onto the stairs leading down to the main entrance.

Freedom at last.

He clocked out and left the building. Forgetting about the shadowy image he may or may not have seen.

Nine till Five

2
MONDAY NIGHT

Adam hadn't been working in the office long. It wasn't the type of work hours he was accustomed to—working all night could sometimes take its toll—but it was a job that paid, and that was what he needed at this moment in his life. A separation and child support costs had ruined his savings, so he needed this second job for the extra money.

It had been a busy night, with various elderly people phoning in about one issue or another. He quite liked talking to them, making sure they were okay, and sometimes reassuring them while a carer made their way out to them. Unfortunately, tiredness was at an all-time high, and he was looking forward to a lengthy break.

"Back soon," he told his colleagues.

They simply nodded and waved a hand, the other hand pressing a phone to their ears. Pushing his chair under the desk, Adam ambled to the door and left.

The whole floor was creepy at night, and knowing there was no-one else there, apart from him and three other care call staff, emphasised it. He glanced to the opposite side of the building, the light fading along the long, dull corridor until it becoming pitch black at the other end.

A vague shape appeared at the window looking into another office at the end. Adam stared at it, fixed on the image. Shaking it off as his reflection, for it had to be, he proceeded towards the kitchen.

His footsteps echoed as he walked, creating the impression that someone was following. He half-turned his head so he could see, in his peripheral vision, if anyone actually was, but there was no-one there. He expected as much and shook his head, reproaching himself for being so paranoid.

The kitchen was a decent enough size without being over extravagant. A fridge freezer sat to the left as he walked in, with a vending machine beside it. Both were used frequently by the staff from the top and bottom floors. A hot water tank was attached to the wall beside the sink, providing boiling water to the numerous tea and coffee drinkers. Rows of tables and chairs sat at the middle of the room, with a smaller table off to the side, which housed various magazines, books, and newspaper that staff brought in.

Adam filled his cup with coffee granules and added water from the tank. He took it over to one of the tables and made himself comfortable, grabbing a newspaper that someone had kindly left. Stirring his coffee as his eyes settled upon the front page, he shook his head at the latest celebrity scandal. *When will they learn*?

He could feel his eyes growing heavier and heavier; the words on the page started to blur and his head began to dip forward. He sat back in the chair and tilted his head back, resting it on the wall behind.

Ting, ting, ting.

"Huh?" A noise had apparently awoken him from his nap. He checked his watch to see how long he had been asleep. Fortunately for him, only twenty minutes had passed. He looked around but no-one else was there.

Ting, ting, ting.

It sounded as if it was coming from outside.

He stood up, using his hands on the table to steady himself, still feeling slightly woozy from being abruptly awoken, and glanced over to the nearby window. He walked across to it and looked out. He was met with his own reflection and part of the kitchen—being dark outside and light inside— and he couldn't see anything outside. He leaned forward until his nose was pressed against the glass and screwed his eyes up.

BANG!

Adam started and stumbled back at the sudden thump in front of his face, nearly tripping over his feet in the process.

"What the…" he muttered.

He managed to compose himself and fixed his eyes back on the window. He caught a glimpse of a shape flutter upwards.

"Stupid bird."

He laughed at his own actions and turned away from the window to pick up his cup. He rinsed it in the sink before leaving the kitchen, sitting his cup on top of the water cooler and heading toward the bathroom door.

He pushed the door open and reached his hand in, switching the light on. He continued to the cubicle. Sitting on the pan, he took his phone out to mindlessly browse during his private moment. *Gone are the days when someone leaves a paper in the toilet.* After a few minutes, he heard the bathroom door open. But he didn't hear it swing shut again. He stared at the cubicle door, as if it would somehow provide him with an answer.

Click!

The lights went out.

Through the gap at the bottom of the cubicle door, he could see light spread across the floor from the corridor, but there seemed to be a silhouette intruding on the glow.

Adam held his breath. Not least because of the strange situation he found himself in, not daring to move, but, at the same time, not exactly sure why. After a while, a sudden thought hit him; someone was playing a prank. After two minutes of the awkward stand-off, he had had enough

"Yeah, yeah, very funny. Leave me in peace. I'll be out soon."

The door closed with a creak and Adam sighed. Before he had a chance to reach down and pull his trousers up, he heard a breath that wasn't his.

"Hello?" he called.

No response.

"Can't a guy take a shit in peace?"

A low, husky snarl was the unexpected answer.

"Enough with the bullshit, alright?"

Silence.

The Fire Exit sign fixed above the entrance produced a faint bloom in the darkness of the Gents. It also told Adam that the prankster hadn't gone, for the black silhouette was still there, shimmering on the floor.

Adam stood and yanked his trousers up, fastening his belt. He took a step away from the cubicle door, trying to figure out what to do. The shadow began to extend underneath the partition in an elongated shape, seemingly reaching for his foot. He shuffled away until his back was against the cistern. He focused upon the dark shape, mystified by it. The outstretched shadow stopped just short of his foot.

Time stood still. It was as if the thing was watching him.

Adam wasn't sure what to do, but the decision was taken away from him as the darkness suddenly shot forward, morphed into a disturbing hand, and grabbed his ankle. He could feel the pressure on his lower leg, as if a human hand had latched onto him, but this was not human.

He tried to pull his leg away, but was caught in a horrific tug of war which the shadow was determined to win. Adam let out a yelp as he began to feel a burning sensation where it gripped him. He looked down, but couldn't figure out how it was causing it. The shape didn't have any substance; it was basically just a shadow.

A shadow from his worst nightmare, but still just a shadow.

"Aargh!"

The pain was intense now.

The bathroom door burst open and the lights came on.

"Adam? Are you okay?" a voice called.

The shadow-hand instantly disappeared leaving his ankle with an uncomfortable tingling sensation. He lifted his trouser leg to reveal a hand print wrapped around his ankle. He let the trouser leg fall back down and slid the latch across, unlocking the cubicle door. He limped out towards his colleague.

"Jesus, Adam. Are you alright? What happened?" Ian asked, scrambling to get the words out fast enough.

"Er, I'm not sure. Something was… something was in here with me."

"Something?" Ian replied, confusedly.

"Yeah. I thought it was someone playing a joke but…" Adam pulled up his trouser leg to show Ian the wound.

Ian's eyebrows lifted and his mouth formed an 'O'. "Fucking hell! How did you do that?"

"It wasn't me. I know how this is going to sound, but something—a shadow or… something—reached under the cubicle and grabbed me."

"A shadow?" Ian said, failing to hide his scepticism.

"I know how it sounds, alright! But it was fucking scary. I'm glad you arrived when you did. I hate to think what might have happened."

"We all heard you clear as day. I thought you were being murdered."

Adam stared at Ian as the word sank in.

Murdered.

"Maybe this is what freaked that cleaner out. I heard he was really freaked out," Ian said.

"Maybe," replied Adam, solemnly.

Ian took Adam by the arm and led him back to the office. "Come on. Let's get you to the first aid box and get your leg looked at."

3
TUESDAY

"Another day in this shithole. Yay!" Damien sarcastically muttered to himself as he walked down the stony path to his foreboding workplace.

Looking across into the distance, he wished he was on top of the heather-filled hills. The sky was pale blue without a cloud to disturb it, and the sun would be fully out soon enough to create a majestic day outside. Top of the hill, looking down on civilisation would be an ideal day, but instead he was going to be stuck indoors, fixing people's PCs. *Joy!* Maybe there would be more creepy stories to make his day more interesting.

He didn't necessarily believe all the ghostly stuff, putting it down to people's overactive imaginations, but the supernatural had always fascinated him. Maybe it was the task of finding proof—or not, as the case may be—that interested him so much. The desire to prove it, one way or the other.

Buzzing himself into the building with his security fob, he clocked in and made his way up the stairs, again using his fob when he reached the door at the top.

Arriving at his desk, he slipped his jacket off and over the back of his chair and slumped down, letting out a loud sigh. He leaned his head back, staring up at the ceiling, as he waited for his machine to boot up.

"Morning," a voice said. "Alright this morning?"

Damien turned to see his supervisor passing by. "Morning. Yup, all is good in the world." The statement was dripping with sarcasm.

His supervisor didn't reply, but smirked on the way out the door.

The machine had booted up.

God! Finally.

The morning rolled on through a haze of password resets and non-existent problems customers created for themselves. He finally had enough and locked his computer, grabbed his coffee cup, and made his way to the break room.

On his way, he decided to have an extended break and headed downstairs to the *big* kitchen instead. It wasn't necessarily a huge kitchen, but it was certainly bigger than the tiny room on the upper floor, *and* it had tables and chairs.

The place seemed quite busy, if the chatter that Damien heard along the hall was anything to go by. Upon entering the kitchen, he saw there were several people huddled round a table, and one man sitting down with his leg rested up on a chair in front of him. His trouser leg was rolled up to the knee.

Everyone turned and smiled at Damien, then carried on their conversation. Damien smiled back and offered a reserved, "Morning," to them all, then quickly turned to the sink to wash his cup.

His curiosity was piqued, however, and he couldn't help but listen to what was going on.

"Wow, that's one hell of a mark…"

"It was a *shadow* that did it?"

Now Damien was really curious. He turned while drying his cup. "I'm sorry for being nosey, but I couldn't help overhear what you were talking about. What's happened?"

"Adam here was attacked last night," said a woman whose name escaped Damien.

"Attacked? By who?" he asked, more intrigued than ever.

"More like, by *what*?" someone else offered.

Damien frowned. "Huh?"

Adam ushered him over and showed him the mark on his ankle. Near enough a perfect hand print was wrapped around it. Adam told him what had happened.

"Ha-ha, yeah! Good one!" Damien said, trying to keep a straight face.

Adam's face remained stoic, though. "No, seriously."

Damien couldn't think of a suitable reply without it coming off as sarcasm, so instead he smiled and nodded awkwardly before returning to the sink to finish making his coffee.

The chat resumed as if Damien hadn't interrupted.

Damien turned to the kitchen exit and glanced over to Adam and the others. "See you later."

They turned collectively. "Bye."

He couldn't get the story out of his head on the way back to his desk. It sounded very far-fetched, but the mark on Adam's ankle was certainly a mystery. No sooner had he got back to his desk than something in his peripheries caught his attention. Through the archway, Nina was waving him over.

He put his cup down and walked across to her.

"Hey, Nina. What's up?"

"Did you hear about the guy in Care call?"

"Erm… no. What?"

"Well, apparently he was attacked by something last night, right here in the building," she said, unable to sit still for the excitement coursing through her body.

"Ah, yeah. Adam. How the hell do you know about it?"

Nina tapped her nose several times. "I have my sources."

Damien chuckled. "More like you're a nosey bugger."

"That as well," Nina replied.

Damien continued, "I just saw him downstairs. It's a bad mark he has on his ankle, but his story is a bit wacko."

"That's the second strange thing that's happened this week… so far," she said.

"I'll be honest with you, Nina, I don't normally believe this kind of stuff, but these incidents have been pretty interesting."

"You're telling *me*. Anyway, that's all I wanted to tell you."

Damien laughed as he turned and headed back to his desk. "Let me know if your nose finds out anything else."

"Will do."

He sat staring at his screen for a while, the stories from the past couple of days replaying in his mind.

What the hell is going on?

*

The afternoon didn't provide much to get excited about for Damien. He'd completed his work early, and he kept thinking about Adam's ankle injury. Opening the web browser on his machine, he decided to check out the history of the place in which he worked. He knew it used to be an asylum in the olden days, but that was about it.

It took a while to find the place. The web had millions of pages of information on various outlandish subjects, but he struggled to find anything about Monreith House. He was about to give up when a web link at the bottom of the screen caught his eye.

Mystery of Monreith.

He clicked on the link and browsed the details. There wasn't much in the way of information, just loose details about a fire and that some patients were, at the time, unaccounted for. He found himself moving closer to the monitor as the read the page.

An image flashed up, causing Damien to jump in his seat, but then the image was gone again, leaving him staring at the screen in amazement.

Bloody ghost stories getting the better of me.

He shook his head as he tried to picture the image—a face—in his mind's eye. It had come and gone so fast, he hadn't discerned much. Long, scraggly hair, and what looked like a manic grin. That was all he saw.

He laughed nervously at himself and shut down the web browser. He went to type up some notes for work when the screen turned black and his machine shut down completely. He looked around at his colleagues, who seemed to be working away without any issues.

He pressed the power button, but nothing happened. Several seconds later the office lights went out, and his colleagues' machines all shut down. Everyone looked confused, turning to each other for answers that wouldn't come. A couple of people cheered, for it meant they had an extra break.

Damien's heart began to beat faster.

The nominated personnel in such an event as a power cut went off to see what the issue was. *Probably a tripped switch as usual*. It wasn't a rare occurrence.

Damien started chatting to Rod, who was seated closed to him. It wasn't long before the lights came back on. The staff came back into the office, laughing and joking about the old wiring in the building and how it was about time the shithole got an upgrade.

Damien watched them return to their desks, then turned back to his own machine. He stared at it, willing the face to appear again.

He laughed at his own overactive imagination.

Nine till Five

4
TUESDAY NIGHT

It was a perfect night. There were no clouds in the sky, and the moon was full, casting a luminous glow over the various buildings scattered around the grounds of the Business Park. A slight breeze rustled the trees.

Billy and Greg loved nights like this for taking photos; they could really pick up some good, atmospheric pictures. They had been to other locations in town, and had picked up some good snaps, which were then sold for some decent money.

Their plan was to get some more of that action tonight.

"Look over there," Billy mumbled, pointing to the right.

Greg was a little bit behind, and couldn't see what Billy was looking at. But then he caught up and saw it. "Dude, that's awesome."

They were in the garden area of the grounds, which featured a pond and a small bridge; a place of tranquillity and beauty, surrounded by trees, flowers, and plants. The moonlight was bouncing off the pond, and they found the whole scene magnificent. Billy and Greg got down on one knee, aimed their cameras, and began shooting.

"What a great night for this. Can't believe we haven't thought about here before," Greg said.

"It's not exactly the place to be wandering about at night. If you believe the stories," replied Billy.

"Lucky we don't, then." Greg glanced across to Billy. "I mean, they're not going to let mental patients wander about in the dark, are they?"

A cool breeze caught Billy's neck and he looked around. "Yeah, I suppose you're right. What happened to that woman was a one off and they *did* catch the guy."

"Exactly. Now stop worrying and just think of the cash you'll be raking in."

Billy couldn't help but smile at the thought of getting paid. "Come on, let's move on."

They let their cameras dangle from their necks and headed over the bridge to the bottom of the gardens. There was a small path that joined a lane running parallel a football pitch further ahead of them. The lane was big enough for a car, but it was all clear tonight. Billy and Greg made their way towards the pitch. Adjacent to them was the main road that led into town. The lane and the road were separated by a tall metal fence.

Their footsteps echoed as they traversed the lane. Billy kept turning around to check, for he thought he heard someone following.

"What's with you?" Greg asked.

"Huh? Nothing." Billy kept his eyes forward, resisting the temptation to look back again.

Halfway past the football pitch, Billy glanced across the opposite side. A row of small trees separated another road from the pitch. The moonlight was at an angle which cast an ominous shadow behind the trees. Billy thought he saw something.

There appeared to be an extra shadow, looking slightly out of place, beside one of the saplings. As if a figure was lurking.

"Er… Greg?" Billy said hesitantly, turning to his friend.

"Yeah?"

"I think I see someone."

"Eh? Where?"

Billy turned back to where he thought he saw the figure and pointed. "Over there."

Greg looked over and screwed his eyes up to try and enhance his vision. "I don't see anything."

Now Billy couldn't see it either. "Shit, I must be seeing things."

"Ha! You must be. Come on, a few more pics then we can get out of here. Scaredy-Cat." Greg began to laugh.

"Fuck you," Billy replied.

Billy's eyes kept returning to the pitch as they continued their journey along the lane. Soon they arrived at a bend leading up to a church.

"There it is," Greg said, excitedly. "The way the moonlight is hitting it, we'll get some brilliant photos."

They hurried along the new cobbled road the corner had led them to, towards the ominous-looking building, eerie in its luminescence. They stood, cameras poised towards the front double-doors, catching the immense structure in the camera's viewfinder, and snapped several pictures.

"Over there. Let try and get the full length of the church," Billy said, moving so he wasn't face on and could see the rest of the building.

Spotlights littered the ground around the base of the church, casting bright lights up its side.

"Hey!" Billy shouted suddenly.

Greg turned in surprise. "Jesus, Bill, you almost gave me a heart attack. What are you shouting for?"

"There… There was someone over there," Billy replied, pointing towards the rear of the church.

"Not again, Billy. You should get your eyes tested."

"No, seriously," Billy said as he grabbed his camera. "Look, here."

He flicked through his recently taken shots and stopped on one that showed the huge building in all its glory, the spot lights doing an excellent job of highlighting it. Greg examined the picture and noticed, right at the bottom right-hand corner by one of the distant lights, there was a darker shadow, blurred, as if someone had been caught on the move. "You mean there?" He pointed at the smudge.

"Yeah, it was only when I moved my camera away from my face, I saw a dark shape moving."

"It certainly looks like something. C'mon, let's go investigate."

Before Billy had a chance to object, Greg was wandering across the grass verge towards the shadow's last location. Billy took an anxious look around him and followed his friend, rushing to catch up.

Arriving at the spotlight in the photo, Greg stopped and looked around. "Hello?" he said loudly, breaking the silence of the night. They both waited for a reply but were disappointed.

"Is someone following us?" Billy asked Greg, trying to sound braver than he felt.

"I dunno. Maybe someone is playing a prank. It's not as if we are trespassing or anything. Anyone can come here for a wander about," Greg replied.

A noise startled them from their conversation. Like something scraping on concrete; the kind of noise that cut right through you, like fingernails down a blackboard.

"What the fuck was that?" Billy asked.

"I don't know but it sounds close. Let's go around here." Greg pointed to the back of the church.

They trod carefully, so that whoever was there couldn't hear the grass scrunching beneath their trainers. They reached the corner and stopped, eyeing each other apprehensively. Greg brought up three fingers and silently mouthed a countdown. They both knew what to do. Billy's heart hammered in his chest. Upon reaching zero, they both jumped around the corner, hoping to catch the culprit.

No-one was there.

Billy blew out a big sigh of relief, his heartbeat beginning to reduce to a normal pace. The atmosphere was somewhat deflated, now that no-one had been found. There was nowhere nearby a prankster could have run to, as open ground surrounded the church. Except for a few trees, but they lay further afield.

Standing on the spot, they searched the near-vicinity for any signs of an intruder, but found none. Greg cast his eyes back to the rear and noticed a set of steps at the opposite corner to where they now stood. From the angle he was at, he couldn't see where they led.

He stepped away from Billy and headed towards them.

"What do you see?" Billy asked.

Greg ignored him and continued towards the steps, stopping in front of them. "This is the only place they could have gone." He pointed towards a metal door at the bottom of the steps.

Billy wandered over and sidled up next to him. He took out his smartphone and activated the flashlight app, shining the white light towards the door. "Look here."

Greg crouched slightly to get a better look, and noticed some light scuff marks arcing outwards to the side of the step. He ran his fingers over the marks and could feel an indentation in the concrete. It had obviously been worn down over time. That was the only explanation he could come up with for the scraping noise they had heard.

Greg turned to Billy and said, "Who would be going into a church at this time of night?" He straightened up and took the corner. He looked up at the windows. "There's not even any lights on inside."

"I don't know, but this is freaking me out. Let's get out of here," Billy replied, turning to walk away.

"Just wait a minute." Greg went back to Billy and stepped up to the door.

Billy stared at his friend with a look of astonishment. "Greg," he whispered, his voice laced with nerves.

Greg held up his hand to shush Billy. He was right beside the door and moved his head closer to it, placing his ear against the cold metal. The breeze had died down somewhat, and the trees had stopped rustling. It was as if the whole environment had suddenly held its breath. All Greg could hear was his own heartbeat thumping in his chest.

Bang!

Greg jumped at the sudden noise and stumbled down the steps, landing hard on his arse. He remained seated in shock, eyes wide and staring at the door.

Billy took a step towards him and knelt to help him up. "You okay?"

Greg shook himself out of his daze. "Yeah… Yeah, just got a fright, that's all."

Billy laughed nervously, although it was more due to nerves than humour. "You and me both," he said, tapping his chest to try and calm his heart.

They both startled to giggle before a sound sent a chill down their spines and stopped them dead.

A faint noise at first, but it was certainly coming from beyond the door. It sounded like laughter but there was an evil, mocking tone to it. It gradually got louder, at which point Billy and Greg knew they weren't imagining it. They looked at each other incredulity.

Greg spoke first. "I don't know what the fuck that was, but let's get the hell out of here."

"Finally!" Billy exclaimed.

They picked themselves up and backed slowly away from the door. The laughter had now stopped, but that made it even creepier; it was as if the source of the laughter was now watching them.

When they deemed themselves far enough away, they turned and fast walked along the road, back to where they had parked the car. Neither Billy nor Greg said a single word or looked back, seeking the safety of their vehicle before mentioned the incident that had terrified them both.

*

Back at the church, the door inched open and the scraping sound—likes nails down a chalkboard—returned as the door brushed the step. A dark shadow was cast across the steps.

Lucky for Billy and Greg, they weren't around to hear the words that followed.

"Come back soon, piggies."

Then the door scraped shut again.

5
WEDNESDAY

Damien had some renewed vigour going into work, as the events from the previous day were firmly still in his mind. That face on the screen, it had looked like a homeless person who was extremely pleased with themselves. Then the power cut. Total coincidence, had to be. But then there was Adam. There was certainly no denying the mark on his ankle. He seemed stable enough that he wouldn't do it to himself, and he seemed genuinely freaked out by the experience.

He had already planned his work day out as he entered the building, and it definitely didn't involve anything that his manager wanted him to do. His sole task for the day was to find out what the hell was going on around here. He especially wanted to run a test, see if that freaky face appeared on his screen again when he visited that same site, although he doubted it.

He was beginning to think he was going crazy. The more he thought about it, the more the details seemed to blur, and he couldn't tell the difference between fantasy and reality.

As Damien started up the stairs, he heard the door open behind him and turned to see who it was. It was Ian from Care Call, heading towards the clocking out machine. "Hey Ian."

Ian looked up to see who had called. "Oh, hi, Damien."

"Say, was Adam working last night?" Damien asked.

"No he wasn't. He called in sick. Don't blame him, to be honest."

"Yeah, me either. Certainly some strange things going on around here, that's for sure."

Ian half-heartedly smiled. "Pfft, yeah. Can't say I've ever experienced anything, but my imagination is certainly in overdrive."

Damien retreated a step down the staircase, eager to press Ian for more information. "Did you know the cleaner that left?"

"Kinda. Max was his name, and he always popped his head in to speak." Ian began to laugh. "Sometimes he never shut up, but he seemed harmless enough. Something must have properly got to him for him to act like that."

"You weren't on that night?" Damien asked.

"No, thankfully. Anne was on, though. You should speak to her about it."

"Cheers, Ian, maybe I will. Is she in today?"

"Yeah, day shift."

Damien turned to finish his ascent up the stairs. "Cool. Take it easy Ian."

"You too, Damien. See ya," Ian said as he headed for the exit.

Damien sat at his desk waiting for his computer to boot up with a smile on his face. Things were certainly rolling along nicely with regards to this little mystery.

Anne was a new source of info. She had actually been on when the cleaner was found, so she could, hopefully, give a good account of what had happened. He would need to time his break right to catch her in the downstairs kitchen while she was on hers. Thankfully, he had worked here long enough to know where people would be and when.

First, he decided to search for the weblink he had found yesterday. He fired up Internet Explorer and typed in what he thought he remembered the name to be: *Mystery at Monreith*. Several hits appeared. He was onto the fifth search page of Google before deciding to start again.

This is useless. He tried different search variations; *Monreith Asylum*, *Asylum Mystery* and several more, but found nothing. This was the *World Wide Web*, and it had returned nothing of interest with regards to the building in which he worked.

Surely I didn't imagine yesterday afternoon, did I?

He could still picture the face and there had definitely been a power cut. He gave up. Slumping back in his chair, he directed his eyes to the clock and realised it was time for his, hopefully, informative break. Grabbing his cup, he locked his computer and left his desk.

As he buzzed the security door leading to the ground floor, he tried to focus his hearing on the kitchen, which wasn't too far away. Various voices spilled out into the corridor but he couldn't hear Anne. He made his way into the kitchen anyway and rinsed his cup, exchanging pleasantries with the other staff members present. He left his cup on the drainer and decided to go and chat shit with the receptionist while he waited for Anne to appear.

The reception was at the start of the corridor and was sectioned off by a door with several small glass windows on either side. The door also had small square windows in, so he could keep an eye on people coming and going from the kitchen. As he made his way to the reception door, a distant voice stopped him.

Be back soon, just taking ten minutes.

Anne.

Damien turned before his hand had settled upon the door-handle and saw Anne rounding the corner at the far end, a mug and jar of coffee in hand.

"Hey, Anne," he called.

"Hi, Damien."

He headed back towards the kitchen and was thankful that everyone else was just leaving. He grabbed his cup off the drainer and started drying it with a nearby tea towel. Anne stood beside him, emptying the dregs from her mug.

Damien turned to her. "Anne, I was speaking to Ian this morning and he said that you were working the night the cleaner went loopy."

Anne returned his gaze. "I wouldn't call him loopy but he was certainly hysterical. Something had definitely spooked him, that's for sure."

"Did he say what?" asked Damien.

"A lot of it was ramblings, but he did mention he felt like he was being watched. And something about the shadows coming to get him. He also said he heard laughter, but the poor guy bolted just after that."

Damien took in the information. "Have you seen or spoken to Adam?"

"No, but Ian told me what happened. Pretty weird stuff going on."

"What do you make of it all? Are people just getting freaked out over nothing?" Damien pressed.

"I don't know but it's an old building. And, with what this place used to be, I wouldn't be surprised if there was some bad aura left behind."

Damien snorted a little. "Come on, you don't really believe that, do you?"

"All I know is that Adam and Max are sound guys, so something serious must have happened to get them in the state they are in."

"Hm, yeah," was the only reply Damien could muster.

"Why do you ask?" Anne enquired.

"Curiosity is getting the better of me. Let's just say I find the whole thing intriguing, I'm trying to piece it all together."

"Just go in with an open mind and be prepared for things you don't understand. There's no telling what you might find. Sometimes things are best left alone," Anne warned.

"Yeah, yeah, I know, but I can't stop thinking about it. I feel I need to investigate."

Anne turned to head out of the kitchen. "Okay, on your head be it. Take care."

And with that, Damien was left on his own in the kitchen with Anne's words ringing in his head.

Some things are best left alone.
On your head be it.

6
WEDNESDAY NIGHT

During the day, Billy and Greg's courage had returned, for they were safe at Greg's house, although the incident from the previous night was still fresh in their minds. Now, as darkness began to fall, Billy's courage waned a little. They had discussed it over and over, until they had managed to convince themselves their imaginations were playing tricks on them. Billy still wasn't one hundred percent convinced, but maintained his bravado in front of Greg.

"So, we're going back tonight, yeah?" Greg asked.

"Er… really? I don't remember agreeing to that," Billy replied.

"Come on, man. We can take the video camera and check out the church again. Get some shit on film."

"And if it wasn't all just in our heads?" Billy asked, nervously.

"Well, we can sell that shit to someone whose interest it piques and make some cash. Get some ghost hunters in on the action. Grab your jacket and torch and let's go."

"I don't know, Greg," Billy said, avoiding eye contact with his friend. "This is exactly how those bullshit horror films start out. Curiosity does no-one any favours. Someone is going to find our asses getting killed on camera."

"Jesus, you watch too many films. You know films are make-believe, right? Like fairies and Santa."

"Ha-ha, funny guy! Course I do, I'm just saying."

"Well don't. It was probably just someone having a laugh at our expense. So, get your shit together and let's get a move on. It's not as late tonight, anyway, so there should be more people about, in case you need to scream for help." Greg could barely contain his smile. For all the horror films Billy watched, he was quite a pussy.

Billy grabbed his jacket, slipping a torch into the inside pocket, and pulled the front door closed. "Yeah, you're probably right."

They walked down the drive to Greg's beat-up VW Golf and climbed in, closing the doors to the cool evening air.

They parked closer to the church this time; Greg stopped the car near the front entrance and turned the engine off. They sat in silence, watching the church, which looked more foreboding than it had last night. Scanning the surrounding area, Billy noticed it was devoid of human life. Devoid, in fact, any life at all. He expected to at least see some rabbits hopping about. "So... where is everyone?"

Greg was still gazing out the driver's window. "I don't know, but we can't be the only ones here."

"Yeah, I'm not sure whether that's supposed to comfort me or not," Billy replied, his voice tremulous.

Greg reached into the back seat and picked up his video camera. Putting it in his lap, he switched it on to check the batteries. "Fully charged," he muttered, as he switched it back off. "C'mon, let's go."

Billy stared at him, glanced over to the church, then back to Greg and sighed. "Okay, let's do it."

The cold air bit into the bare skin of their hands as they closed the car doors and looked over to the church entrance. There were no lights on inside the church.

Same as last night, Billy thought. *Doesn't mean no-one is in though.*

Greg already had the camera pointing at the door and swung it round in a slow arc to pick up the expanse of land surrounding it, trying to catch anything untoward.

So far, so good. Billy had a slight tremble in his arms, but couldn't decide if it was nerves or the cold. He was thankful he wasn't operating the camera, otherwise they would get nothing decent.

They edged towards the building, ears pricked for any unusual sounds. Greg held the camera to one side, still facing the church, and pointed with his other hand. "Let's go around the back," he said quietly.

They slowly walked along the road that skirted the chapel. They were now standing in the same place as last night, at the rear of the church facing the metal door.

They hesitated, each waiting for the other to make the first move. Turning to face each other, Greg spoke first. "It was my privilege last night. Your turn tonight, Billy boy."

Billy sighed and bowed his head. *It's only fair*, he thought, before speaking. "Okay, just keep your camera close by."

Greg tapped the camera and gave a thumbs-up.

Billy shuffled towards the steps leading down to the door, like a teenager in a strop, glancing back at Greg with nearly every step he took. Greg inched closer as well, keeping his camera trained on the door rather than Billy. Billy stopped in front of the metal entry and took another look back at Greg. Greg ushered him on with his hands, and mouthed the words: *Go on.*

Billy turned back to the door and hesitantly placed his ear on the cold surface. He held it there for what felt like a lifetime, but was really no more than twenty seconds. His heart was pounding and his breathing grew rapid. He was sure, any second now, something would thump against the door on the other side.

Nothing happened. No-one banged on the door or laughed a manic laugh.

"What now?" Billy said, moving his head away from the door, and stepping back.

"Luckily, someone has come prepared," replied Greg, reaching into his pocket and pulling out a torch and penknife. "Here, allow me." Greg sat the camera on the corner of the step, still recording their every move. He aimed the torch towards the edge of the door and ran it up and down, looking for any small groove he could put his fingers in to try and prise it open. Towards the bottom he found one.

It was big enough that he could slide his fingers into, so he tucked the knife back in his pocket. His fingers didn't go far into the depression, but enough that he could pull the door, or at least try to. Adjusting his stance, he pulled as hard as he could. He felt it move slightly. "It's definitely moving."

"Let me try," Billy said, moving towards his friend.

"On you go, Mr. Muscle," Greg laughed.

Billy adopted the same stance as Greg and pulled with all his might, his faced turning a beetroot colour in the process. The door opened further this time, grinding against the stone steps, the noise shrieking through the lonely night. Billy jumped back as he was met with darkness beyond. He pulled his own torch out and switched it on, casting light into the dark. "We're in."

Greg bent down to pick up the video camera and, standing beside Billy, he said, "You ready?"

"Not really. Breaking into a church isn't exactly going to earn us good karma," Billy responded.

"After what happened last night, we need to check this shit out."

Billy looked around him. "Maybe, maybe not."

Greg frowned. "Let's go."

He edged Billy aside and took up lead position at the entrance, torch and camera pointing inwards. The light illuminated a narrow alley and another door at the end, this one wooden. Greg and Billy took slow, gradual steps towards it, Billy turning around every couple of steps to point his torch towards the exit. Greg stopped at the door, and Billy nearly bumped into him. They listened for a few seconds.

Silence.

"Turn your torch off," Greg told Billy.

He did as he was told and Greg did the same, plunging them both into complete darkness, all except for the faint gloom from the entrance behind them.

Greg grabbed the door handle and turned it slowly, gently pushing at the same time to see if it would open. It moved inwards without noise, so Greg pushed it further until there was enough space for him to enter. He took a step forward and poked his head around the door.

Even though it was pitch black, he could make out the vague outline of shapes. They were long and appeared to be in rows. This was the nave, Greg realised. Glancing around, he saw windows, which, on the outside, were the ones sitting high up along the outer walls.

The moonlight failed to fully penetrate the gloom. Though, at the back of the room, he could make out an altar.

Billy jabbed Greg in the ribs, like a petulant child eager to see something he thinks he's missing out on. Greg turned to him and pulled an angry face, putting a finger to his lips, urging Billy to keep quiet. Billy rolled his eyes and looked away.

Greg examined the nave again, fully expecting someone to move or make a noise. When he was as sure as he could be that they were alone, he turned to Billy and mimed for him to switch his torch on. Billy happily obliged while Greg did the same.

Two beacons of lights cut through the darkness in swathes as they moved around the large area, casting shadows which danced around. They stepped fully into the room and closed the door behind them.

"Well, there's no-one here and nothing strange going on, so I guess you were right. It was just someone playing a prank. We can sleep easy now," Billy said in a hushed tone.

Before Greg had a chance to reply, a noise at the back of the church caught their attention. They quickly brought their torches up in one fluid motion and aimed them towards it, and were just in time to see a door, leading to another room behind the pulpit, slowly swing shut. It didn't fully close, as there was a slight gap where it had bounced back open. The mystery person was obviously in a rush and had been too busy scarpering to ensure it shut fully.

"Okay, dickhead, we know you're there," Greg said loudly, his voice echoing around the high ceiling. "You can come out now."

There was no response.

Greg and Billy shared a glance before Greg turned away and started walking towards the door.

"Whoa, whoa. Where are you going?" Billy asked, almost becoming tongue-tied.

"I'm not letting some little shit get the better of me. Especially when we have him cornered." Greg continued towards the door.

Billy swung the torch around, illuminating the dark corners in case their tormentor was not working alone, as he followed Greg.

Greg didn't even hesitate when he reached the half-open door; he lifted one foot off the ground and kicked it in. Discretion was no longer an issue. The door swung inwards and crashed against the wall. Greg already had his torch and camera pointing into the small room before the door had a chance to swing shut again.

He stuck his foot out to prevent it from going any further then stepped in. Leather-bound books ran up to the ceiling, stacked on shelves lining the edge of the room, and a desk sat behind the door with a chair neatly tucked underneath. There was, it appeared, nowhere for anyone to hide.

"No-one here," Greg announced with a puzzled look on his face. "Nowhere to go either."

Billy entered the room. "Maybe it was the wind."

Greg glared at him.

"Okay, okay, maybe not," Billy conceded.

Greg wandered across to the desk and, after a cursory examination, decided there was nothing of interest. The drawers in the desk were locked. Billy walked by the bookcases, shining his torch on the titles. All God and church related, *surprise surprise.*

He turned to speak to Greg and, as he lifted his foot, it caught upon something, causing him to stumble. The torch fell from his hand and clattered on the floor as he grabbed hold of one of the shelves to steady himself. The light went out suddenly as the torch hit the ground, the batteries falling from the case and scattering.

Greg turned and stared at his best friend. "What the fuck are you doing?"

"I tripped," Billy replied, catching his breath as he grasped onto the shelf.

Greg pointed his torch onto the ground at Billy's feet. "Well, well, well, would you look at this?"

There was a rug that was now crumpled up, thanks to Billy's foot, but it was what was underneath that interested Greg.

What looked like a wooden trapdoor was cut into the concrete floor. Greg bent down, grabbed the corner of the rug, and whipped it away, letting it land in a heap by the desk. It definitely was a trapdoor. There was no handle, but a small depression had been cut into the stone to allow a hand to grab hold of it.

Greg placed the video camera on the desk so that it faced the hatch and went back to examine it, passing his torch to Billy.

Billy looked shocked. "What the hell are you doing?"

"What does it look like?" Greg replied.

"Whoever it was, never went down there, did they? How the fuck did they manage to get the rug back across it, huh?"

Greg stopped for a moment, a quizzical expression upon his face. "Well, let's take a peak anyway."

Billy didn't have a chance to protest before Greg yanked up the hatch and placed it gently on the floor. The dust floating through the torchlight looked like stars twinkling in the sky. Greg took the torch from Billy. He stood on the cusp of the hatch and peered down into it. It seemed to be about eight feet deep, and there were steel footholds stuck into the wall. Dropping onto his haunches, he aimed the torch further in. It was a lot deeper than he had initially thought.

"It looks like it leads to a tunnel."

Silence.

"Billy?"

As Greg turned to look at his friend, something struck him on the head, sending a flash of white across his vision and pain shooting through his body. He wobbled slightly, trying to refocus his sight, when he was struck again, this time sending him falling forwards into the opening. He lay still, struggling to grasp what had happened. His half-opened eyes remained blurry but, thanks to the way the torch landed, he could make out two dark figures above him.

"Welcome, little piggies," one of the figures said in a gravelly voice.

Before Greg had a chance to even register the words, one of the dark shadows seemed to grow larger as it moved toward him.

A heavy weight landed on him and then he closed his eyes and he drifted off into oblivion.

"… more meat to mangle," a random voice finished saying.

Greg didn't catch the start but he was glad of it. His head throbbed worse than a bad hangover and he found he couldn't move his arms or legs. Panic coursed through his body and he began to shake. He gradually opened his eyes but it took a while for them to adjust to the gloom.

"He's awake," another voice said, hoarse but filled with excitement.

"What? Where am I?" Greg mumbled. "Who are you?" He could make out some figures close by.

"Billy?" he suddenly remembered. "Where the fuck is Billy?"

A voice to his left said, "Don't you worry your pretty little head about your friend." Then there was a faint laugh.

As Greg's vision grew accustomed to the gloom, he started to take in his surroundings. Three men stood in a half circle in front of him, parting ways to allow him to see what lay behind them.

Several feet in front of him stood a stone structure, like a makeshift table, and on top of it, in each corner, were candles. What his brain couldn't grasp was the body lying on top of the table, its head twisted over to the left-hand side at an impossible angle. It looked like it was struggling to stay a part of the body. Buckets lay beneath the improvised table, and they appeared to be filled with a dark liquid. Greg abruptly recognised the clothes and his heart sank. He let out a whimper.

"Billy?" he said quietly, lips quivering. "No, no!" Tears began to fall down his face and he tried his best to break free from his restraints, but failed.

A horrible, deranged laugh rang out.

"What the fuck do you want?" Greg screamed. "What… do you want?"

A man stepped forward, but through the gloom Greg couldn't make out his features. "Your soul. That is the gift you will give us. Our friends in the shadow world need it to grow stronger, and in return we get life." He sniggered. "Immortality."

Greg, for some strange reason, giggled, his brain starting to fragment under the fucked-up situation he now found himself in. "Help, help!" he yelled.

"It's no use; no-one can hear you. We made sure of it."

Turning away from Greg, the man pointed to the table and barked instructions at the other two men. "Get rid of him." He turned back to Greg. "And prepare this one."

When Greg had first looked at the table, he thought the body was in one piece. He now knew that wasn't the case as they started to drag Billy's limbs off the table. Shaking with fear, he felt bile rise in his throat. A second later, from his mouth spewed the contents of his stomach. He coughed and spluttered as, finally, nothing more came. The men moving Billy didn't even look up, didn't even acknowledge him, just simply shifted Billy's hacked-up body off the table.

The man in charge came close to Greg's face. Greg could now make out bloodshot, manic eyes, a beard spattered and sticky with some sort of fluid and dirty, mud-covered skin. He looked down at the floor. "That nearly hit my foot," he growled.

Greg was about to instinctively look down when the man punched him in the side of the head. White stars shot across his vision and his head fell forward, his chin coming to rest on his chest. He willed the pain to subside. His eyes closed.

When he opened them again, Greg couldn't comprehend what was happening. The scenery had changed, for he was now staring at a dirty ceiling. He looked left and right and realised he must have blacked out, as his arms were now outstretched and tied down. He tried to lift them but nothing happened. He did the same with his legs, but they too were secured. He tried to rest his head back but found there was no surface to place it, so he leant it back as far as it would go.

The upside-down face of the bearded man met his gaze.

"Wakey, wakey, sunshine," the bearded man said, and laughed.

Greg stifled a scream in his throat.

He lifted his head up as far as it would go, and that was when he saw the other two men at the bottom of the table by his feet. He started breathing hard and fast, praying that his heart would give out before whatever happened to Billy, happened to him.

He rested his back again and began to plead with the maniac behind him. "Please, please, you don't have to do this."

"Oh, but I do." The man crouched down so his face was right in front of Greg's. His breath was redolent of rotten meat. "What seems like a lifetime ago now, I was locked up. Like an animal. Treated like shit. Tested on. It was there that I discovered a higher power, and that very same power helped me escape. It couldn't help everyone, but, I now owe it and, in return, I and several others will have our wishes granted."

Greg spat in the man's face. "Fuck you, you crazy bastard."

The bearded man lifted his arm, which Greg now saw was horribly burnt, and wiped the spittle from his cheek. He disappeared from view and returned with a book that looked old and leathery. He opened it and flipped it upside down. He then smiled at Greg, before nodding once to the two men down by his feet.

Greg couldn't help but follow his line of sight, but quickly wished he hadn't. He saw that the men now held sharp objects in their hands. They weren't brand new shiny, but the candlelight reflected off them all the same. He noticed the rusted teeth at the bottom of each instrument and, with his last ounce of energy, he tried again to break the restraints, to no avail.

He sobbed to himself and wailed, wishing he had listened to Billy in the first place wishing they had never come to this hellhole. They could have been at home right now, supping on beers.

The men drew the tools across each of his upper thighs. A line of blood began to dribble down onto the table, and he screamed with all his might.

The bearded man laughed and stared menacingly into Greg's eyes. "This may hurt a little," he whispered.

He then proceeded to speak in a language that Greg had never heard before, looking up to the ceiling and closing his eyes as he did so.

His assailants began to dig the rusty tools into the wounds, sawed at them, forcing them through flesh before they became stuck in bone. Greg's screams and howls echoed around the room. Before one leg was severed fully from his body, he had passed out.

He was oblivious to the rest of the suffering his body would endure over the coming moments.

7
THURSDAY

Damien was dying to tell someone about the spooky shit that was going on at work, and the only people he could think of were Grant and Nina. They already knew a little bit and he couldn't wait to fill them in on the rest. He wondered if he could convince them to stay late the following night with him; perhaps they could conduct their own amateur investigation. Might take some convincing but he'd ask.

The sun began to blind him as he drove to work while his mind wandered. He glanced to his left and saw the large church that stood nearby; in the opposite direction, there was just fields and hills.

The scenery is so lovely, but the traffic is a bloody nightmare.

He parked the car and signed into work on autopilot, a routine he'd been through for more years than he cared to admit.

He ambled over to Grant and Nina's cubicle. "Morning, my fellow happy workers."

They turned and spoke in unison. "Hey, Damien. What's happening?"

"Nothing much…" he couldn't contain it until later. "Except we work in a place that used to be an asylum. Where there was a massacre... and a fire. And in the past week, some strange shit has been happening." There it was. All out.

Nina spoke first. "Well… that explains the cheery atmosphere around this place."

Grant laughed.

"Anyway, do you fancy working late tomorrow night to help me out? I'm going to have a little look around," Damien said.

Grant looked gobsmacked. "A look around? In the dark? After the lovely bit of exposition you just gave us? You're fucking mental, mate. There's no way, you're on your own."

Damien turned to Nina. "And you?"

"Erm… as tempting as you make it sound to spend a night here, I'll politely decline," Nina answered.

"It won't be all night," Damien added.

"Oh, well that's alright then." Nina rolled her eyes. "It's still a no from me."

Damien looked deflated. "Suit yourselves, your loss. This could be a right adventure."

"It won't be if you end up dead," Grant said.

"Funny, mate, funny," Damien replied, and started to walk away. "You need to work on your sense of humour."

Dead? Pfft, whatever.

Damien sat himself down at his workstation, wondering what exciting plans his boss had for him.

*

The morning passed by quickly thanks to the fuckwits who couldn't properly operate a computer.

Honestly, how many times do I have to show them?

Before Damien knew it, it was lunchtime. His growling stomach indicated it better than any clock ever could. He glanced out of the window to see what the weather was like. It still looked bright, maybe even warm, but at least it wasn't raining. He decided to take a small walk before going to the café on the opposite side of the car park for a chicken and BBQ mayo wrap. Locking his machine, he stood up, put his jacket on, and walked downstairs to the exit.

As he thought, it was mild outside, with just a few clouds dotting the sky. Damien unzipped his jacket a little and took to the road. He didn't plan on going far; round by the church, then along the road that led to the back of the small eatery. It was a short loop that made him feel less guilty about the overindulgence of chocolate that often happened in the afternoon.

Taking in the expansive greenery, his eyes wandered back and forth over everything. It was a peaceful place to be. Looking back at Monreith, he frowned and struggled to make sense of the strange phenomena that had occurred there.

How could something so abnormal happen in such a harmonious setting. He shook his head, as if it might reset his mind and banish the unsettling thoughts. He looked over in the direction the road took him, and his eyes settled on the church. It wasn't the church itself that held his focus, but the figure in dark clothing sitting on the bench outside.

As he drew closer, he saw that the man was elderly, with a bald head on top and thin wisps of hair scattered around the summit. He wore thin-framed glasses, and seemed to be fixated on something on the ground that Damien couldn't see.

Damien approached. "Hello there."

The elderly gentleman visibly started, as if someone had shocked him, and a split second later Damien heard something land on the grass with a soft *thump*.

"Oh, oh, you startled me," the man said, leaning over to pick up the object.

As the elderly man turned towards Damien, he noticed the dog collar peeking out from under his jacket.

"Sorry… Father," he said. It seemed the right thing to say. "I didn't mean to scare you."

"It's okay, son. I was in a world of my own."

The object, which Damien could now see clearly, was a video camera. Damien pointed towards it and said, "Is it okay? Not damaged?"

"No, no, it's fine. Just some mud and grass in places," the vicar replied, wiping it clean.

There followed an awkward moment of silence between them, seemingly hanging there.

Damien broke first. "Do you mind if I sit?"

"Of course not." The vicar gestured for him to sit.

"I'm Damien, by the way," he said, extending his hand.

The vicar did likewise. "Father Jones."

"I hope you don't me saying, but you seemed quite captivated with the video camera," Damien commented.

The vicar stared at the device solemnly before turning to Damien. "That would be one word for it. I found it." He must have caught Damien raising his eyebrows. "Now, I wouldn't normally look at someone else's private thing, *but* where I found it… well, it left me quite speechless."

"Er… okay. Would you mind telling me where?" Damien asked.

He stared at Damien as if debating whether to tell him or not before he finally spoke. "When I finish for the evening, I walk around the inside, making sure all the doors are closed and everything is in its place. I leave, and I always lock the church behind me."

Damien wondered where this tale was leading. "Okay."

"This morning, I come in, everything is as it should be. I open the door to my office and find it sitting on my desk, just sitting there facing away from the door.

Everything was exactly the way I left it and the front door was still locked."

"Well, that certainly is peculiar," Damien said. "So, if you don't mind me asking, what was on the video?"

The vicar let out a sigh, removed his glasses, and wiped his forehead with the back of his hand before handing the video camera to Damien. "See for yourself."

Damien took it, and immediately began searching for the *play* button. He eventually found it and watched in silence.

There was a man leaning into what looked like a pit, a torchlight sweeping from side to side. Then a figure suddenly appeared behind him. The figure struck him and he disappeared into the opening. It then turned and picked up what appeared to be another body, and threw that in as well. A gravelly voice said, "Welcome, piggies". Then a trapdoor was shut and the rest of the video played out in darkness. There was sound, but no visual, and noises could be heard. It sounded like something material being dragged, soft footsteps, and then a door slamming shut.

"Jesus Christ!" Damien said, somewhat automatically and forgetting his company. He turned to Father Jones. "Sorry, Father."

The vicar nodded his head in forgiveness.

"Have you checked the pit?" Damien asked.

"No, I daren't touch anything. I've been sitting here most of the morning, wondering what to do."

"You need to take this to the police," Damien exclaimed.

"I will, I will." Father Jones looked slightly confused. "I just don't want the Lord's house swarmed with people. They'll turn the place over looking for evidence."

Damien sighed. His mind started ticking over, and an idea came to him. "How about… we both go check? We could just lift the lid and look in?"

"I don't know," the vicar said, glancing at his watch. "I have a meeting to attend in Edinburgh tonight. I'm sorry, but I need to get sorted. It was nice meeting you, and I'm sorry to have troubled you with this." He stood to leave.

"Tomorrow night!" Damien blurted out. "I need to work late tomorrow night. I could come over; I only work over there." He pointed across to his work building. "One more day and we could have a little look together. If we find anything, we'll contact the police. Will you be back?"

"Yes, I will be back. But, why are you so interested?" the vicar asked.

"There have been some unusual thing happening at work. Nothing like this, but almost... *otherworldly*. It just seems strange that this has happened here, so close, and in the same week. Maybe coincidence, I suppose."

"Otherworldly?"

"Yes." Damien's eyes darted up to the sky. "And not in the good way."

"Oh. Oh, right. I suppose leaving it one more day couldn't hurt," the vicar replied, zipping his jacket fully up. "I'll meet you here at seven pm."

Damien noticed more clouds had gathered in the sky.

"Okay, Father. See you then."

With that, the vicar nervously scuttled away, eventually disappearing around the corner of the church.

Damien stared at the ground, his mind going over the videotape he had just watched.

Coincidence, pure coincidence, Damien told himself.

He felt the first drops of rain as the sky darkened. He zipped his jacket up to his chin and jumped off the bench, fast-walking to the café to get his lunch.

8
THURSDAY NIGHT

Ronald pulled into the car park and searched around for an available space, which he found just a moment later. He made sure his security tag was in his pocket before leaving the warmth of his car, and zipped his jacket up as he made his way toward the building that would be his new place of work for the foreseeable future. At least until he could find something more permanent. Spending the day playing video games and watching films, and working just a few hours at night, had been enjoyable while it lasted, but he felt he needed more direction in his life.

Tomorrow. A new start tomorrow.

Arriving at the main entrance, he took the tag out of his pocket and swiped it across the sensor. A green light appeared and he pulled the door open.

The cleaning materials sat in a locked cupboard off to the right of the entrance. He rummaged in his trouser pocket for the key given to him by the admin staff, located it, and proceeded to unlock the door to begin his work.

Swinging the door open and looking at the items inside, he thought that this wasn't that bad a gig: replace the toilet rolls and hand towels, mop the floors and vacuum the offices where necessary. He could cope with that. Since he started work after most of the office staff had left, he was allowed to listen to a radio while he worked, so he had brought along his Bluetooth speaker which he could connect his phone to.

Happy days!

He decided to start downstairs this evening, as he knew that the care call staff would be about. The only downside was, he wouldn't be able to play his music down there. The hand towels were all wrapped together in a large bundle, so he grabbed the first one and carried it to the fobbed door leading through to the bottom section of the building. He buzzed the door open and nudged the hand towels across with his feet to hold it in place.

Returning to the cleaning cupboard, he dragged the vacuum out into the corridor then went back and picked up the mop and bucket, took them to the same place.

Ronald started to fill the hand towel dispenser in the kitchen to start with, and it was then that he heard approaching footsteps.

"Hi there," he said chirpily when the man entered the room.

The man returned a smile. "Hey. So, you're the new guy, huh?"

"That's me. First night on the job. The name's Ronald."

"Pleased to meet you, I'm Ian."

Ian sat at the nearest table and grabbed one of the magazines someone had discarded during the day. Ronald finished with the dispenser and shut the case which a *click* that seemed to echo. He felt a strange sensation wash over him, as if he was being watched. He turned to find Ian staring at him.

"Everything okay?" Ronald asked.

Ian stuttered for a moment before replying, "Erm, yes, yes. Sorry, I don't mean to be rude." He looked down at the magazine with a sheepish look, then back up to meet Ronald's eyes. "Do you know about the last cleaner?"

Ronald frowned. "No. Why do you ask?"

"No reason. Anyway, I best get back. Nice meeting you."

"Yeah, you too."

Ian went to leave but turned before reaching the doorway. "If you experience anything strange, don't hesitate to give us a shout. And I do mean *anything*."

"Erm… yeah, sure," Ronald didn't know what else to say.

Ian left before Ronald had a chance to question him, and he listened as the man's footsteps faded along the hallway.

Ronald was left wondering what the man had meant. "Strange? What the hell do you mean by strange?" he muttered to himself.

He finished off his jobs on the bottom floor, satisfied with a job well done. He still couldn't quite shake off Ian's weird statement, though. Strange as in supernatural? It was a big building, so maybe Ian was referring to the possibility that it was haunted.

He chuckled to himself and laughed off the notion, believing that any ghostly occurrence could be rationally explained. He accepted that some people believed in such things, but it wasn't for him.

He finished the ground floor in decent time so moved upstairs. After lifting the vacuum cleaner to the top of the stairs, he went back to collect the rest of the items he required. He buzzed into the secure door and propped it open with a mop bucket. He moved all the items through and stacked them next to the water cooler, which could be located halfway along the corridor. It sat between the Ladies and Gents toilets, and opposite the tea room, so it was a handy central place to start. He still had the main and smaller offices around the far end of the building to do as well, but those tended to need nothing more vigorous than a light vacuum.

Ronald sat the speaker on top of the cooler and pulled out his smartphone to connect to it. In a few seconds, a thumping bassline was audible, and someone was boasting about women and money.

He went into the Gents first to refill the hand towels and toilet roll, exited, then stood in front of the Ladies. He wasn't sure if anyone was in there, but he decided to play it safe.

He put one hand on the door and knocked gently with the other. No response. He pushed it open slightly. "Hello," he called out. Still no response. He entered and proceeded to repeat his task.

As he was in the first cubicle, he thought he heard a noise over the music from the speaker. He stuck his head out of the cubicle, found nothing untoward, and went about his task.

But the noise returned as he went back to refill the toilet rolls. It sounded like someone gently knocking.

Shit, maybe someone needs in.

He opened the main toilet door and stuck his head out, expecting to be met with an impatient woman. There was nobody. He looked left and right. Definitely no-one there. He re-entered the room and finished his duties. He could hear his music playing and gave a little shimmy towards the exit. He was enjoying his job so far—left on your own, no office workers to get in the way of and no rush.

Excellent.

Completing his jobs in the toilets, he went through to the main office to see if anything needed done. He took the speaker with him, picking it up off the cooler and heading through the door at the end of the hall. The corridor was lined with frosted windows on the office side, so Ronald could already see that someone had left the lights on.

He opened the door and entered. He sat the speaker on the nearest desk, leaving the music playing, but turned it down slightly in case someone he couldn't yet see was working at the far end.

The office was open-plan and his music echoed around the room; it seemed to bounce off the high curved ceiling and spread throughout. Pods of four and five desks scattered the floor space; an archway led through to the other side. From where Ronald stood, the same floor format was replicated throughout. The only difference being, the other side was in darkness. The light from his side illuminated the first couple of meters, but then waned, leaving the rest in pitch black.

Beside the entrance door, Ronald noticed a large, half-full bin. He lifted the lid off and took out the black bin bag, setting it on the floor. He quickly checked beneath the desks to see if there were any bins which needed to be emptied, but found none. As he stood up near the last pod, something moved just beyond his vision.

He turned and looked through the archway, but couldn't make out anything out of the ordinary. He watched for several seconds, standing stock still. He eventually shook his head and laughed to himself, cursing Ian for trying to spook him. He headed back to the bin bag, tied it in a knot at the top, and put it out in the corridor, ready to be taken to the recycle bin outside.

He walked towards the archway to check the bins on the other side, and was almost there when the music from the speaker started to distort. It was as if the tempo had slowed down, as if the artist's voice had become robotic.

"What the…"

He turned back and walked towards it, picked it up and checked it over. Not seeing anything obvious, he switched it off and back on again. He connected his phone back up and pressed *Play*. The music started normally. Ronald made his way back to the archway again and, upon reaching the same place as before, the music did the same thing. He stopped and looked back.

Maybe the phone is too far away to connect properly.

He went back a second time. As he picked it up, the lights in the office went out.

"Shit!"

Ronald stood motionless in the dark, unsure of what to do.

He stepped cautiously over to the light switches and switched them all off and on multiple times.

Nothing happened. He noticed the hallway lights were off as well.

Great! First night on the job and there's a power cut.

He stood still, debating what to do.

There should only be one bin through the archway anyway. Then I'm done.

For a third time, he headed towards the archway, wondering what else could go wrong. Making it successfully through without incident, he decided it was a waste of time searching under the desks for bins, as he couldn't see much. As he searched around, though, he was sure he saw a black shape cutting through the darkness. It appeared to be pitch black, making it stand out against the gloom. Ronald looked directly at it, but the more he stared, the more his sight blurred and he couldn't tell whether it was inside or outside the office.

"Hello?" he called.

There was no answer.

"Hello?" he tried a second time.

Still no answer.

A thought came to him; hit him like a bolt of lightning. A smile crept across his face.

Ian.

All his talk of experiencing strange things, Ronald knew what this was. Prank the new guy. "Very good, Ian. You nearly had me there," he shouted.

He continued his hopeless bin-finding quest, ignoring Ian standing over by the door. "You know, it's a good trick to pull, Ian. A less stable man might have been shitting himself by now. I must say, good effort," Ronald said, moving slowly around the office and no longer paying attention to the door.

He was at the pod opposite the door when he looked over to see that Ian was no longer there. Ronald chuckled to himself and made his way to the same door where Ian had stood. There was a bin sitting there. He pulled out the bin bag, tied it at the top, and went to leave. As his hand touched the handle, the lights came back on in the office and out on the corridor.

"Thanks, Ian," he called. "That's much better."

Dumping the bag by the door, he turned left and headed through another door. This one led to some smaller offices.

This must be where the managers sit, away from the riff raff. He giggled at his own joke.

Making his way between the offices in search of more bins, he found one in the end office, which was overspilling with empty crisp packets and cans. Picking it up, he made his way back to the corridor, where he'd left the large bin bag. As he walked, he felt something on his bare arms, a breeze.

He put the bin down and went into each individual office to check for open windows. He couldn't remember seeing any, but he would double-check. Once he was satisfied that none were open, he went and stood where he had initially felt the breeze. He determined it was coming from a door which stood slightly ajar off the hallway.

He pushed the door fully open and found himself in a stairwell. He could still feel a breeze on his skin, so he followed it down the stairs until he located the problem.

Some idiot had left the alternate exit door wide open. He made his way towards it and stepped outside. Strangely, there was no wind and no-one about. Ian certainly had pulled out all the stops in order to scare him.

Behind the door stood a short wall, and behind the wall he noticed another door. It, too, was slightly ajar. Stepping fully into the night, he had a front view of the building. It certainly was a large structure. Rows of windows littered its frontage, allowing Ronald to glance into it.

A long corridor ran the length of the building, connecting both ends. As he looked around the complex, his gaze fell upon a window at the far side, which would have been either the Ladies or Gents toilets, if his memory served him correctly. The window was frosted and glowed, as it a faint light shone beyond.

A very human shape stood there, bathing in the glow.

Because the glass was frosted, he couldn't make out details, just a shape against the light. A silhouette which scared him far more than it probably should.

Nice try!

A noise to his right startled him, shook him from his trance. He looked over to the open door, took another look around, and then proceeded over to it. He had no clue what this door was or to where it led, but someone must have opened it. Doors don't just open on their own.

Ronald edged the door further open with his foot and peered inside. He stepped forward onto a concrete floor and another set of steps, these ones leading down. His heart started to beat faster as he stood at the top of the steps, stared into oblivion, his nerves beginning to make themselves known.

A dark void awaited him, but he spied a metal rail attached to the wall beside him. Taking hold of it, he gently placed a foot on the next step. Convinced this was still a prank perpetrated by Ian, or someone else trying to freak him out, he plucked up some courage and soon arrived at the bottom step.

He couldn't see anything, just a wall of black in front of him and a dim rectangle glowing at the head of the steps behind him.

"Hello? Anyone there?" he called into the dark.

Silence was the only response.

"Fuck this," he muttered, turning to make his way back up the steps.

A faint laughter stopped him in his tracks as one foot was on the journey upwards. He half turned, deciding he had had enough of Ian's games. As he took another step up, the door at the top slammed shut, causing him to jump. Now, he couldn't see anything, and had to feel for the steps with his toes. "Fuck you, Ian, this is beyond a joke now!"

He made it up two steps before something latched onto his ankle and pulled. Before he knew what was happening, he began to fall forward. The suddenness of the attack caught him by surprise, and before he could put his hands out to protect himself, his head cracked off a concrete step. Stars shot across his vision and his head ignited in pain. He lay still, eyes fluttering.

Suddenly, he was being dragged down and away from his safe haven. His head clattered off each step, and it hurt like a sonofabitch.

Ronald's last thought before he blacked out was what Ian had said earlier:

"If you experience anything strange, don't hesitate to give us a shout. And I do mean *anything*."

He finally understood.

9
FRIDAY

Sleep didn't come easy for Damien the night before. In fact, he wasn't convinced he slept at all. He remembered seeing nearly every illuminated hour of the clock sitting on his nightstand. His mind was too busy racing with the information he had gleaned in the past few days.

Just what the fuck is going on? Are the incident at the church and the occurrences at work connected?

He wasn't sure. Maybe it was just a freakish coincidence.

Maybe.

He barely recalled the monotonous journey to work that morning, and before he consciously took note of his surroundings, he was buzzing himself into the door at the top of the stairs.

"Here he is, our very own ghost-hunter," a voice from the kitchen said.

Damien stopped and made his way back to the door he had just wandered past. "Ugh, you two," he grumbled.

"Good morning to you too, Damien. Wow, you don't look so great," Nina teased.

"Yeah, thanks for the update," Damien returned.

"Cheery as well," Grant chipped in. "What a pleasure."

Damien noted the heavy tone of sarcasm and raised his middle finger in response. Grant and Nina laughed.

"You still hunting ghosts tonight?" Nina asked.

"Sure am. Still time for you two to change your minds and man up." Damien smirked, before adding, "Especially since there is a slight change of plan. I'm going to the church instead."

They both looked gobsmacked. "What? The church? You suddenly found religion?" Grant asked, barely containing his laughter.

"I went for a walk yesterday and ended up talking to the vicar. Turns out he had a strange story of his own. Someone left a video camera on the desk in his *locked* office and the footage was—" Damien coughed, "—weird, to say the least."

Grant and Nina exchanged a puzzled glance. Grant spoke first, "So… what was on it?"

"There appeared to be this… this hole in the floor, and someone was looking into it. Then there was a bit of commotion, a scuffle I think, and it went dark. Then there were some footsteps and a door closing. I think somebody's still down there."

"Shit. Why didn't he take it to the police?"

"He didn't want the church getting overturned for the sake of what might be nothing. Plus—"

"Plus?" Nina encouraged.

"I kind of persuaded him to hold off for a day so that I could help him investigate first. That's what I'm doing tonight. There could be someone down there. Or a fucking body or something."

"Fucking hell," Grant exclaimed. "This is turning into something from a *Most Haunted* episode."

"I don't know who's crazier, you for going or the priest for letting you," Nina said.

Damien laughed nervously. "Yeah, it kind of has escalated a bit. They're probably not connected anyway. Probably just some kids mucking around." Damien raised his eyebrows at his colleagues. "The offer is still open…"

"Yeah, okay" replied Nina.

Grant's mouth dropped open as he stared at her, Damien likewise. "Sorry, what was that?"

Nina looked as cool as a cucumber. "It's not as if it's actually a ghost. Like you say," nodding at Damien, "it's probably just some kids who broke in, mucking about. Anyway, an extra pair of hands would be better if they come back tonight. Grant?"

Grant looked shocked. "No chance, not on your nelly. Do you realise the craziness of what you just said? You were more scared of something imaginary than of someone who could *actually* hurt you."

"I can't kick a spirit in the nuts if it attacks, now can I? And someone has to look after Mr Muscle here, and the priest."

"And that person has to be you?" Grant asked.

"And you…" Nina replied, giving him her best puppy-dog eyes.

Grant shook his head vigorously. "Sorry, but no. You should just phone the police."

Damien spoke up. "We will, just not right now. Straight after, I promise."

With the conversation over, they all left the kitchen together, heading back to their desks. Damien looked at Nina and smiled, before nodding in Grant's direction. Knowing what Damien was getting at, she shook her head and shrugged her shoulders.

There was no changing his mind.

Damien waited until later in the day to catch up with Nina, while Grant wasn't about, and arranged for the night ahead. He agreed to pick her up at six-thirty then head across to meet the vicar.

This was going to put some much-needed excitement in his life.

10
FRIDAY NIGHT

He couldn't believe what they were about to do. *Maybe* this was wrong. *Maybe* they should just phone the police and let them deal with it. *Maybe* he should just forget about the strange happenings at work and carry on as per usual. *Maybe*. Fear had started to creep in. What if they found a drug stash? What if the dealers were still about and decided not to leave any witnesses. Damien's mind raced.

"You okay?" Nina asked.

"Erm, yeah... yeah," Damien replied, keeping his eyes firmly focused on the road ahead in case Nina saw the doubt in his eyes.

"You're unusually quiet, that's all," she added.

Damien let out a small giggle. "I have my moments, you know."

Nina didn't reply. Damien's eyes never wavered from the road.

"That's us nearly there. Are you sure you want to come along? I can easily drop you back at home," said Damien.

Nina looked at him. "Hey, we are just looking. If we find anything, we pass the info on to the police." She continued to eye him with a smirk on her face. "Anyway, an extra pair of fists will come in handy if someone has come back. We could make a citizen's arrest."

Damien burst out laughing, welcoming the humour at a time when he had been considering turning around and heading back. "I'm sure it won't come to that, Wonder Woman."

She jabbed him in the ribs and laughed.

"Hey, watch out," he teased. "That's us here. Wouldn't be good luck if we crashed into a church, now, would it?"

"Sorry," Nina said sarcastically.

Damien stopped the car at the side of the church and looked around for the vicar. There were no other cars about, not nearby, anyway. He saw headlights in the distance, veering off in different directions.

Late worker, he thought, *nearly seven pm on a Friday, Christ.*

He looked at the church and mouthed *Sorry* silently. He would need to stop taking the Lord's name in vain, especially so close to His house, *and* not while the vicar was around.

He checked his watch—7:10pm. "Where the hell is he?"

"Maybe he decided to take the video camera to the police after all," Nina said, echoing Damien's thoughts.

"Shit, I hope not. There's some weird stuff going on around here and I want to know what it is."

Nina turned to face him. "Why does it bother you so much?"

"Curiosity. I don't know why, but I can't stop thinking about everything. I need answers before my brain can take a break." Damien looked at her. "Sounds weird, right?"

"Yeah, kinda," Nina replied, laughing. "I can understand it, though. Dog with a bone springs to mind."

Damien laughed as well. "Yeah."

A few minutes of silence passed between them, both stuck with their own thoughts before someone decided to speak. It was Damien. "This might be him." He was looking in the rear-view mirror, watching the approach of a set of headlights.

Nina turned as well. The car pulled up and parked close behind them, the lights were killed, and the driver emerged. Before Nina could say anything, Damien had already stepped out of the car, ready to greet the newcomer. "Hi, Father. I wasn't sure if you had changed your mind."

"No, no. Although it did cross my mind. I'm just back from Edinburgh." He looked around Damien to the figure in the passenger seat. "Someone else tagging along?"

Damien looked round. "Oh, yeah, I hope you don't mind, but I mentioned the video to a friend at work and she wanted to provide some assistance, you know, in case the culprit comes back"

Father Jones stared at Damien for a few seconds before saying, "That's fine. The more, the merrier."

Nina got out of the car and walked over to them. She looked at the vicar. "Hi, I'm Nina."

The vicar smiled and nodded. "Father Jones."

"So," she said, "shall we get this show on the road?"

The men looked at each other and nodded in silent agreement.

They made their way over to the church, Father Jones taking the lead as he rummaged in his pockets for the keys to the door. As he fit the key in the lock, he pivoted to face Damien and Nina. "You know, maybe we should just leave this to the police."

The surprise on Damien's face was more than obvious. "We're here now, Father. Just a quick look then we can go."

Father Jones glanced back and forth between Damien and Nina, then sighed. "Okay, if you insist." He turned the key and pushed open the large door.

Damien and Nina entered first and marvelled at the size of the auditorium.

"You've never been in before?" Father Jones asked, struggling to contain a smile at their child-like expressions as they looked around.

"No," Damien replied, seemingly in awe.

"Nor me," Nina added.

Father Jones chuckled. "If you carry on up the steps, then go straight ahead between the pews, my office is at the back on the left-hand side."

The dull moonlight coming through the high windows lit the place up ever so slightly, creating an eerie effect where pockets of darkness were scattered throughout. Nina moved a half step closer to Damien. "No lights?" she asked.

Father Jones ignored the question and stepped past them. "Follow me."

Nina looked at Damien. Damien returned the look but simply shrugged and followed. Trailing behind the vicar, they cast their gaze warily over the pews, keeping vigilant for anyone that may be lurking. They were so busy focusing that they nearly bumped into Father Jones, who had halted at a door.

"Here we are," he said, and opened the door. "This is where I found the video camera." He pointed at his desk. "It was facing towards the back wall."

They followed Father Jones into the office. Damien searched the wall for a light switch. He found one and flipped it on. Light illuminated the small, windowless room, momentarily dazzling them all. Damien blinked several times and stepped forward, immediately spying the rug. He extended his foot and flicked a corner back.

"Woah!" Nina said.

"Woah, indeed," Damien replied. "You ready?"

Nina swallowed what she really wanted to say. "Yeah." Perhaps she sensed that it was too late to change her mind.

Damien saw an indentation around the edge of the trapdoor and reached for it. He dug his fingers in to get a good grip and pulled hard. It lifted easier than he thought and swung open. He rested it on the floor behind them.

Damien peered over the edge and could just about make out a dusty floor at the bottom, thanks to the angle of the light seeping in through the office windows. He also noticed small metal bars jutting out from the concrete wall.

"Nina, come over here and look at this," he said.

"What is it?"

He motioned with his hand. "Come over."

Nina took a few steps forward and looked over the edge. "Okay, good, there's nothing there. Can we go now?" She retreated as quickly as she could.

"These look like steps," Damien said, pointing toward the metal bars.

"And?" She was clearly unnerved about the whole thing now.

Damien raised his eyebrows and smiled.

"Uh-uh, no way. A look and that was it. You agreed, remember?" She shook her head. "Father, are you good to call the police now?"

She waited for a response. None came. "Father?"

She half-turned to see where he was when something thumped into her back. She lost her balance instantly, and fell towards the hole in the floor. It took Damien a second to register what was happening, by which time it was too late, Nina was already on her way through the opening.

Before he could do anything, something hit him, too, and he sprawled forwards. His world turned upside down and he landed with a smack on his back, his head smashing against the hard ground. Nina was now beside him, nursing her arm. "Damien? Are you okay?"

He tried to lift his head a little. "What the fuck happened?"

The both looked up to see Father Jones' silhouette in the trapdoor, staring down at them.

A second later their world turned black with a loud bang as the trapdoor slammed shut.

*

Father Jones turned away from the trapdoor and dragged his desk over the top of it to prevent them from attempting to escape. The office door creaked open and a large shadow was cast across the floor.

"Well done, Father," a voice croaked.

The vicar didn't bother to lift his head to see who was there. He knew who it was. "Just don't leave any evidence this time. The video camera was sloppy. Lucky it was me that found it."

"Watch your tone with me," the voice said, menacingly. It was closer now, even though the vicar hadn't heard any footsteps. Suddenly, hot breath hit his face, a rotten stench of meat that had gone off. He still didn't raise his head. "Your kind have been helpful over the years, but just remember… I can strike you down in an instant and make your pain last. Your God won't help you."

Father Jones winced at the threat but attempted to keep up his bluster. "And who would serve you then?"

A menacing chuckle erupted in the room, throaty and gruff. "We have others, more than willing."

A shadow suddenly moved across the floor and the door slowly creaked shut. Father Jones heaved a big sigh, his hands shaking upon the desk. He crossed himself, even though he knew it was useless.

It always *had* been.

*

"Father? Father Jones?" Damien called up to the trapdoor. No answer.

"Come on! What. The. Actual. Fuck!" he screamed, but there was still no response. His body began to shake with panic.

Nina put a hand on his arm and he flinched, as if touched by a red-hot poker, momentarily forgetting he wasn't alone. "It's just me."

"Phones," Damien suddenly said, using his hands to frantically search for his mobile. "Have you got yours?"

Nina searched as well. "Yeah, it's here," she said, unlocking the screen.

"What a surprise… no fucking service." She switched on the flashlight function instead.

A bright light illuminated Damien and the wall behind him. He was now sitting upright and checking his phone. "Shit…same here."

"Damien, your head."

Damien looked at her confused, then reached his hand round and felt for the wound that was causing his head to throb. He found the stickiness first, and then a gash. As his fingers explored it, a shooting pain reverberated around his skull, causing him to clench his eyes tight, hoping it would fade. It subsided eventually, but the dull ache of the injury could still be felt.

"What the hell did Father Jones do that for?" Nina asked. "He's a vicar, for fuck's sake. A vicar! And he's going around pushing people into—" she looked around, pointing her phone in every direction, "—what looks like a basement."

Damien didn't have an answer for her. "I don't know."

He clambered up onto his feet and wobbled slightly, putting his hand on the wall to steady himself. He followed the light over to the metal bars and put his left foot on it. He proceeded to climb up until he could reach the trapdoor. He pushed, but it didn't give an inch. It had been locked. Up there, on the other side of the trapdoor, he could make out two voices, but not what they were saying.

Damien felt the frustration rise, and he began to hammer on the wooden obstacle. "Fuck!" He gave up only when he could hammer no more, and his head started to throb.

It didn't take long.

Then he heard whimpering. He pointed his phone at Nina, who now had tears running down her face and her body was shaking. He climbed down the bars and went to comfort her.

"Fuck off, Damien." She pushed at him with her good arm. "Why didn't you just let him take the fucking video to the police? Huh?"

"I'm sorry," he said, taking a step back. "After what just happened, I don't think he would have."

"Yeah, but we wouldn't be stuck down here, would we?" She wiped her nose with her sleeve. "I could be at home right now, having a bath and relaxing with a glass of wine."

Damien remained silent this time, not wanting to be on the receiving end of another rebuttal. He felt guilty about the whole situation, and couldn't blame Nina for hating him.

There came, from somewhere close by, a maniacal laughter. It was barely audible, but Damien heard it.

"What the fuck?"

Nina looked up at him. "What? What is it?"

"Shh," he said, waiting for another period of hush. "Do you hear that?"

She turned her head this way and that, trying to hear what Damien could. "No, I don't hear anything."

Damien pointed his phone past her at the floor, which disappeared into the distance. It wasn't a chamber at all, but some kind of tunnel.

He stepped past her, his phone at arm's length in front of him. The ceiling remained high enough for an adult of average size, and the passage of worn bricks maintained its width until the phone light was consumed by darkness.

This has to be man-made. Damien thought.

"Nina?" He turned to look at her. "If this is a tunnel, there must be an exit somewhere."

Nina took a second to wipe the tears from her face. "But why would the vicar push us down here if there is an escape route?"

"Again, I don't know. But, we need to do something, and it looks as though this is the only way." He lit the tunnel up with his phone once again. "Come on."

He took Nina's hand and helped her to her feet. She held out her phone alongside his as they slowly made their way into the unknown.

*

The tunnel went in a straight line for a while, the bricks of the walls getting dirtier and grimier as they went on, the air getting thicker and more claustrophobic. They came to a couple of corners they had to take and carried on. Nina was so on edge and out of her comfort zone that the slightest noise, imaginary or real, caused her to check over her shoulder.

"There, look," Damien said, pointing into the darkness beyond the barrier of their lights. "I think I can see something."

Nina screwed up her eyes. "I can see it too; I just don't know what it is."

"Neither do I, but it's the first sign of *something* we have seen for ages, so that's a good sign."

"Hopefully," Nina said, warily.

As they were about to continue, a noise behind them stopped them in their tracks. It sounded like someone was scraping metal across bricks.

They looked at each other and gradually turned around, expecting the boogeyman to be standing right there, staring at them. But there was nothing illuminated in the glow from their phones.

"Hello?" Damien called.

They held their breath in anticipation.

Silence was the answer.

They breathed out.

Damien could feel his heart hammering in his chest, and Nina grabbed hold of Damien's arm. They turned back around and the sight before them stole their breath away.

A man stood there, his face partially illuminated by the glow of their phones. He had long, unkempt hair and a straggly beard—all the attributes of a homeless person. Only this homeless person was grinning evilly. "Hello, piggies."

Nina screamed but before Damien could react, the man grabbed him and smashed him over the head with a hard object. His internal lights went out immediately, body falling to the dirt.

Nina turned to run but her foot slid on the ground as she went to take off, costing her vital seconds. Another man appeared from seemingly nowhere and pounced on her as she scrambled in the filth. He grabbed her head and slammed it forward into the dirt. Her vision began to blur and darkness closed in.

Another blow to the head was all it took to knock her unconscious. She lay lifeless.

The hobo-looking man grabbed Damien's oxter and lifted him up, holding onto him. He looked at his accomplice and said, "Bring her."

*

Damien's mind swan aimlessly in pitch black as voices drifted in and out of his consciousness.

Open your eyes. Open your eyes. Softly, gently.

"Huh?" he mumbled.

"Open your eyes!" a voice screamed, followed by a demented laugh.

Damien's eyes shot open, darting around the room. He was so surprised that he couldn't see what was right under his nose, literally. A face obscured his view.

He began to focus; beady, rat-like, bloodshot eyes stared back into his, breath like a bin that hadn't been emptied for weeks washed over him, causing him to gag. The man's skin was covered in dirt and dust and bits of something Damien couldn't even begin to describe stuck to his dishevelled beard.

"Evening, Sunshine," the man growled, not retreating a bit.

"Who… Who are you? What do you want? Where—"

The man slapped him hard across the cheek before he had a chance to finish his question, causing his head to loll to one side. The man gave him a second, the lifted Damien's chin and forcing his head back so that they were eye to eye again. "One question at a time." he said. "*We* are merely servants. What do we want? Well, you'll see soon enough."

Damien's breathing hastened as he tried to comprehend what was going on.

How has it come to this?

His brain was struggling with the fucked-up situation it found itself in. Then he remembered something. How could he forget.

"Ni… Nina. Where is she?"

"Oh," the man said, feigning confusion. "I don't know. Where could she be?"

He stepped away from Damien so he could see past him. Damien's eyes bulged at the sight and he gulped, trying desperately to produce some saliva for his dry mouth.

Nina lay, spread-eagled, on a stone table. Candles sat at each corner, chasing away the shadows, all except one large one that hung from the ceiling above her. The table beneath her was blood- and gore-stained. Damien didn't need light to know what he was looking at.

"Nina," he said. "It will be okay, I promise." Tears began to roll down his cheeks.

The man chuckled, but it was as if the laughter was in surround sound. It wasn't just coming from in front of Damien. As he struggled to turn his head, men appeared on either side of him, laughing loudly.

"It definitely *won't* be okay. *I* promise," he growled, and laughed again. "You're just in time for the main show, actually."

"Nina! Nina!" Damien shouted, trying to free himself from his restraints. It was no use, he couldn't rouse her.

She is unconscious or dead! Dead!

The gruff man walked over to the table and picked up a book which sat on the far side of Nina. He looked back at Damien and smiled a crooked smile. The other two men moved to each of Nina's legs and bent down, reaching under the table, producing metal instruments, which they held aloft over her subdued limbs.

Crazy, these people are fucking crazy! This can't happening! The thought repeating itself like a mantra.

The leader stood at Nina's head, placed his hands on her temples and turned it towards Damien. Damien gasped as he noticed her colourless face, blank, staring eyes, and misshapen forehead. It was like a crater just seeping blood. The man turned the book upside down, opened it, and began to read.

"No! No!" Damien bawled. "What the fuck have you done?"

"I'm afraid Cedric here," he gestured to one of the other monsters, who now held what looked like a saw, "was a bit enthusiastic when trying to restrain her. For her sake, it's probably best."

Damien stared at the beast before him, then moved his eyes between the other two men, before resting them on Nina. He began to sob, his entire body shaking as If in the throes of a seizure, but for his hands and feet that were firmly restrained. He began to scream. "Father! Father Jones! You bastard!"

"Ha, ha! The good old Father," the man tormented. "He has been useful over the years."

Damien's body stilled. "Years? What do you mean?" he asked, confused by the vicar's involvement in this nightmare.

The man turned to face him. "The Father has been at this church for decades, helping us get the pigs to give to the shadows—"

"Pigs?" Damien spat. "Shadows? What the fuck are you talking about, you freak?"

His tormentor glared at him before walking over, grabbing his little pinkie and yanking it all the way back. It snapped and there came the sound of someone stepping on a twig.

Damien let loose a blood-curdling scream.

"Let that be a tame lesson on interrupting," he said. "The Father helps us get people—the homeless, for instance. The sort who won't be missed. This week has been real lucky, though. Two nosey bastards and now you and this lovely young lady. My, oh my, they will be pleased."

"They? Who?" Damien asked.

"They, who are getting stronger with every sacrifice made. They, who already have enough strength to traverse the tunnels down here and make their way into the connecting buildings. Soon, the brightest light won't even stop them. They are from another world. They convinced Father Jones that God doesn't listen, that it would be in his best interests to assist. They can be *very* persuasive." He started to laugh. "Their touch can burn, disintegrate even, so don't piss them off." He finished by rolling up his sleeve to reveal a horrific, infected wound on his arm. The skin had been melted badly.

"No! No way," Damien said, shaking his head back and forth. "This isn't real. It can't be." His mind flashed back to work; Adam and the burn on his ankle. Stark realisation hit him. "Shit," he muttered.

The man chuckled. "Now, where were we?"

He turned back to the table where Nina lay and opened the book again. He began to speak in a language Damien didn't think was possible, and then he nodded to the men at the other end of the table. Damien's eyes flitted over to them in time to see them lift their tools and begin to saw into the flesh on Nina's thighs. Blood began to ooze over the table edge and down into buckets on the ground below.

Damien released the contents of his stomach. Even when there was no more to come, he dry-heaved for longer. He started to feel light-headed; the man's words playing like a record on repeat, lulling him to sleep. He tried to resist but it was useless. He was going.

Before darkness wholly washed over him, he thought he could make out a dark shape above Nina, watched as it detached itself from the ceiling and floated down towards her, spindly tendrils reaching out and plunging into her body.

"Not real, not real," he giggled insanely over and over, his mind fully broken and refusing to believe what his fading sight had revealed to him.

He slipped into darkness.

EPILOGUE

The inmates—though not that anymore, not for a long time—stood in awe as three colossal shadows came down from the ceiling in the sacrifice chamber and stood before them.

They were almost human-shaped, but without any features. Just a misty, shimmering figure. Wraiths. The shadow people.

The inmates stood back, not daring to get too close, not daring to reach out for one touch to see if they had any substance or not.

"You have served us well, humans," the largest figure said, from a mouth that couldn't be seen. "Without you, we wouldn't have been strong enough to enter this world. We have plans for you yet. You will help us bring more of our brethren over to your world."

"Yes, master," the unkempt lead mortal said.

The three figures chuckled menacingly, and then the leader spoke in a voice drenched with malevolence.

"Good. Go forth and wreak bloody vengeance. Your world is about to change forever."

THE END

ABOUT THE AUTHOR

Hailing from the South West of Scotland, Dale Robertson lives with his partner, two children and pet dog.

Growing up, his first taste of horror came from shows such as Eerie Indiana, Goosebumps, and Are You Afraid of the Dark? The first movies he remembers were Child's Play and Aliens, which only enhanced his fascination with all things scary. Reading wise, he was (and still is) a huge fan of Stephen King, Dean Koontz, James Herbert and Richard Laymon (in no particular order!).

As well as being a movie, book and video game enthusiast, he also likes to keep active by playing football, badminton and going the occasional run.

As well as his own work being self-published, some of his other tales have appeared in anthologies and the work of other writers. He is continuing to write and working towards getting more stories out there.

Printed in Great Britain
by Amazon